THE STORM WHALE
in WINTER

With thanks
to Nia, Lara & Jane

Henry Holt and Company • *Publishers since 1866*
175 Fifth Avenue, New York, New York 10010 • mackids.com

Henry Holt® is a registered trademark of Macmillan Publishing Group, LLC.
Copyright © 2016 by Benji Davies
All rights reserved.

Library of Congress Cataloging-in-Publication Data is available.
ISBN 978-1-250-11186-9

Our books may be purchased in bulk for promotional, educational, or business
use. Please contact your local bookseller or the Macmillan Corporate and
Premium Sales Department at (800) 221-7945 ext. 5442 or by e-mail at
MacmillanSpecialMarkets@macmillan.com.

First published in hardcover in 2016 by Simon & Schuster UK
First American edition—2017
Printed in China by Toppan Leefung Printing Ltd.,
Dongguan City, Guangdong Province

10 9 8 7 6 5 4 3 2 1

THE STORM WHALE
in WINTER

Benji Davies

Henry Holt and Company
NEW YORK

Noi lived with his dad and six cats by the sea.

Last summer, Noi rescued a little whale after
a storm washed it ashore. He and his dad
took it back to the sea, where it belonged.

But Noi could not forget his friend.

Now and then he thought he caught a glimpse of the whale, its tail tipping the waves in the distance.

But it was always something else.

Winter was setting in, and all around the island the sea slowly filled with ice.

Noi's dad took one last trip in his fishing boat.

But when darkness fell that evening, his dad was still not home and Noi began to worry.

Noi watched and waited,
waited and watched.

Suddenly, he saw something
out at sea.

It was his dad—it had to be!

He counted all six cats safe inside
and dashed down to the shore.

Noi dragged his boat to the water's
edge, but the sea was frozen hard.

I must be careful! he thought,
stepping out onto the thick ice.

The farther Noi went, the harder the snow fell, until everywhere looked the same.

Noi was lost!

Then up ahead he saw a gray shape flickering in the lamplight.

It was his dad's boat stuck in the ice.
Noi quickly clambered aboard.

"Dad?" Noi called.

But his voice echoed—the boat was empty.

Noi didn't know what to do. As he curled up tight,
he imagined the deep sea swirling beneath him,
and he began to feel afraid.

Then through the darkness, the boat went *BUMP!*

It was the storm whale.
The whole family had come to help Noi.

The whales pushed their noses
into the cold night air.

They sang through puffs of steam and spray
as the ice cracked and crunched.
Somehow they knew where to go.

The little boat thumped hard against the rocks.
"Dad!" cried Noi.

"Noi! What are you doing here?" said his dad.
"I just had to find you!" said Noi.

As winter turned slowly to spring, they often spoke of that cold, icy night.

The night the fishermen had rescued Dad,
and the storm whale had rescued Noi.

And Noi would smile . . .

. . . because it was the night
his friend came back.